Before reading this book  to know:

- two or more letters can represent one sound
- the sound /ae/ can be represented by the VCe spelling <a-e>

This book introduces:

- the VCe spelling <a-e> for the sound /ae/
- text at two-syllable level

Words the reader may need help with:

was, he, for, school, birthday, no, said, the, his, they, she, goal, day

Vocabulary:

shame – when someone is sorry that something happened
blame – say that someone is responsible for something wrong

Talk about the story:

Frank is always late.
One day he is late for a soccer game.
What will his teammates say?

Reading Practice

Practice blending these sounds into words:

came	lake
mate	name
gave	take
shame	state
made	blame
game	wake
cake	save

Late

Frank was late. He was late for school. He did not wake up.

Frank was late for Dad's birthday!

"Shame, no cake left!" said Mom.

Frank was late for the game.

His mates lost the game.

They blamed him.

Beth was upset.

"Take this!"

She gave him a box.

The box had a clock in it!
Frank was not late for the
next game.

Frank saved a goal.

"Frank saved the day!" his pals yelled.

Questions for discussion:

- What happened when Frank was late for his dad's birthday?

- Why were Frank's mates angry?

- What lesson did Frank learn?

Jumping Jack

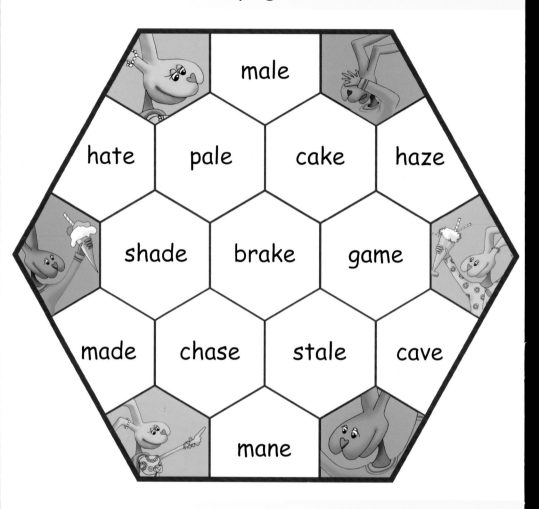

This is a game for two players. Each player has three counters, each set a different color. Players choose to be Frank or Beth and place one counter on each of their characters. Players take turns to move a counter by sliding it into an adjacent space or by jumping over their opponent's counter into an empty space. When a player lands on a word, he/she must read the word aloud. The winner is the first player to get all three of his/her counters in a straight line.